D1228386

Maddie and Mabel
Take the Lead

To Mom and Dad, for being the someones
who are always there. –K.A.

To Nora and Louisa, my favorite pair of sisters –T.M.

Maddie and Mabel is published by
Kind World Publishing, PO Box 22356, Eagan, MN 55122
www.kindworldpublishing.com

Cover design by Tim Palin Creative

Published in 2022 by Kind World Publishing.

Printed in the United States of America.

ISBN 978-1-63894-012-8 (hardcover)
ISBN 978-1-63894-013-5 (ebook)

Library of Congress Control Number: 2022933953

Maddie and Mabel Take the Lead

By Kari Allen
Illustrated by Tatjana Mai-Wyss

Eagan, Minnesota

CHAPTERS

The Friends 6

Bud 14

The Dance 30

The Cookie 46

First Day 60

THE FRIENDS

Maddie and Mabel are sisters.

Maddie and Mabel are friends too.

Maddie likes to be brave.

Mabel likes to watch.

Mabel has lots of ideas.

Maddie tries to help.

Since Maddie is the big sister,
sometimes she does things first.

Since Mabel is the little sister,
sometimes she does things second.

Mabel and Maddie are sisters.

And friends too.

BUD

A tall tree stood in the middle of the yard.

It was Maddie and Mabel's favorite tree.

Maddie and Mabel named the tree Bud because in the springtime the tree had beautiful flowers.

Maddie told Bud all of her stories.

Mabel told Bud all of her ideas.

Maddie and Mabel told Bud their secrets.

And Bud listened.

Sometimes Maddie and Mabel leaned on Bud and watched the clouds together.

Or they listened to the wind dance through Bud's branches.

One day, Maddie and Mabel wanted to climb Bud.

"How do we get up?" asked Mabel.

"Watch me," said Maddie.

Maddie climbed up
to the first branch.

Mabel did too.

“How high are we going?” asked Mabel.

“Until we are high enough,” said Maddie.

Maddie climbed to the second branch.

Mabel did too.

“Are we high enough yet?” asked Mabel.

“Not yet,” said Maddie.

Maddie climbed to the third branch.

Mabel did too.

"When will we stop?" asked Mabel.

"Now," said Maddie. "Now we can stop."

Maddie and Mabel hugged Bud.

Mabel looked out.

Maddie sighed.

“Mabel?” said Maddie.

“Yes?” said Mabel.

“How do we get back down?” asked Maddie.

Mabel smiled.

“This time,” said Mabel, “watch me.”

Mabel climbed down.

Maddie did too.

The Dance

One day Maddie and Mabel heard music coming from somewhere in their neighborhood.

"Let's dance," said Mabel.

"How should we dance?" asked Maddie. "There are lots of ways to dance."

“I like to dance fast,” said Mabel.
“Fast and wild.”

Mabel moved her arms
and kicked her legs very fast.

“That’s not how I like to dance,” said Maddie.

“I like to dance slow,” said Maddie. “Slow and serious.”

Maddie moved her legs and waved her arms very slowly.

They tried to teach each other their dances.

"You're not doing it right," said Mabel. "Watch me."

"I am doing it right," said Maddie. "You're not doing it right. It's like this."

Mabel tried to teach Maddie.

Maddie tried to teach Mabel.

Then the music stopped.

Maddie and Mabel were quiet.

“I liked your dancing,” whispered Mabel.

“I liked yours too,” said Maddie.

“I wasn’t done,” said Maddie.

“Neither was I,” said Mabel.

“There’s no more music,” said Maddie.

“We can’t dance anymore,” said Mabel.

Maddie and Mabel both stood still.

“Maybe we don’t need music,” said Mabel. “Maybe we can make our own.”

“That’s a good idea,” said Maddie.

So that’s exactly what they did.

Mabel and Maddie danced fast and slow, and wild and serious.

And they made their own music together.

THE COOKIE

Maddie and Mabel had a cookie.

"Look at this cookie," said Maddie.

"It is a big cookie," said Mabel.

"It looks like a yummy cookie," said Maddie.

“But there’s one cookie and two sisters,” said Mabel.

Mabel had a plan.

"We will split the cookie," said Mabel. "I will get half and you will get half."

"That is not fair," said Maddie. "What if one half isn't half? What if it is more?"

Maddie had a different plan.

“We will take turns,” said Maddie. “I get a bite, then you get a bite.”

“That’s not fair,” said Mabel. “What if you get to go first and last? What if there are not enough bites?”

Maddie and Mabel had a lot of plans and not enough cookies.

"I am hungry," said Mabel.

"Me too," said Maddie.

"We don't want to waste the cookie," said Mabel.

"No," said Maddie. "That would be the worst plan."

"What if . . ." said Maddie and Mabel together.

"You go," said Mabel.

"What if I split it . . ." suggested Maddie.

"And then I get to pick the half I want first," said Mabel.

"I'll make sure to be fair," said Maddie.

"Me too," said Mabel.

It was a big, yummy cookie,
and just enough for two sisters.

FIRST DAY

It was the first day.

Maddie had her **first** first day already.

Mabel had not.

Mabel needed to know some things.

Mabel needed to know these things so she could be certain on this first day.

So she asked Maddie questions.

Lots and lots of questions.

"What if I don't like it?" asked Mabel.

"You might not," said Maddie.
"But I think you will."

"What if it's scary?" asked Mabel.
"What if it's hard?"

“There might be some hard parts,” said Maddie. “Sometimes the hard parts can be the best parts.”

Maddie thought for a minute and then said, “There might be some scary parts. But most times the scary parts are not really scary once you do them.”

"I'm not sure I can do it," said Mabel.

"Someone is always there to help," said Maddie.

"Always?" asked Mabel.

"Always," said Maddie.

"Like you help me?" asked Mabel.

"Like I help you," said Maddie.
"And like you help me."

Maddie and Mabel walked slowly.

Until there was nowhere else to walk.

Maddie looked at Mabel.

Mabel looked at Maddie.

"Do you want me to go first?"
asked Maddie.

"No," said Mabel.

"Do you want to go first?" asked Maddie.

"No," said Mabel.

Maddie thought.

"Do you want to go at the same time?"
asked Maddie.

"Yes," said Mabel.

So that’s what they did until Maddie stopped.

“What did I tell you it’s like again?” asked Maddie.

“You said I will like it.”

Maddie nodded.

“You said there might be hard parts. But that’s okay,” said Mabel.

Maddie took a breath.

“You said there might be scary parts. But they turn out to be not that scary,” said Mabel. “And you said that there is always someone there to help.”

Mabel stuck out her hand.

“Are you coming?” she asked.

Maddie took Mabel's hand.

"I was right," said Maddie.

"About what?" asked Mabel.

"Someone IS always there to help," said Maddie.

MAKE A KINDER WORLD

In these stories, Maddie and Mabel take turns and practice sharing. When do you share with others? How do you share? Do you take turns? What are other ways to share?

TALK ABOUT IT

What do you do when you are nervous about something new? How do you prepare when you are going to do something for the first time?

How do you teach someone else how to do something you love to do?

CONNECT TO YOUR STORY

Write or draw about a time when you taught someone how to do something. How did you teach them? How did you explain it so that someone else could understand? What was hard about teaching someone? What worked well?